Thin Ice

by Sue Graves and Roger Simó

Chapter 1

It was a very cold Saturday morning.
The ground was icy, and frost clung to the
trees. Pete, the man next door, was out early
taking his dog for a walk. Mum watched as
he slipped on the pavement.

Mum went to the cupboard.

"I'll sprinkle some salt on the path," she said.

"It will make it less slippery."

3

Lenny followed Mum outside and got his bike
out of the shed.

"Where are you off to?" asked Mum.

"I'm going to the woods with Ted," said Lenny.

"Well, be careful, and keep away from the pond,"
warned Mum. "It will be slippery at the edge
and you could fall in. Ponds are dangerous places
in icy weather."

"Don't worry, Mum," said Lenny. "We'll be careful."

Chapter 2

The track was icy and the bikes kept skidding.

Ted's bike spun round. "This is cool!" he yelled.

Next they made a ramp with some logs.

They took turns to speed up it and jump off.

The bikes slid all over the place when they landed.

"This is the best fun ever!" shouted Lenny.

But, after a while, Lenny got bored.

"Let's go to the pond," he said.

"I don't think that's a good idea," said Ted.

"Your mum told us to keep away from it."

"We won't go that near," replied Lenny.

"I just want to see if there's any ice on it."

Ted looked worried. "Well, we must keep away

from the edge."

The pond was frozen over. Someone had nailed

a sign to a post at the side. It said:

DANGER – THIN ICE!

Ted pointed to the edge of the pond.

"Look at that little duck," he said.

"Poor thing," said Lenny, "it wants to get into

the water."

"Let's find something to break up the ice," suggested Ted.

They searched by the pond and found a branch.

"This will do," said Lenny.

Together they smashed a hole in the ice.

The duck jumped in and swam round and round.

Lenny stamped hard on the ice. "It's really thick," he said. "I think that sign's wrong. I bet we could skate on this."

Ted wasn't sure. "We should test the ice first," he said.

Ted picked up a rock and threw it into the middle
of the pond. The rock skittered across the top
but it didn't shatter the ice.

"Told you so!" laughed Lenny. "I was right.
The pond is safe."

Lenny stepped on to the ice and slid over straight away. He spun on his back towards the middle of the pond.

"Nice one," laughed Ted. "Stand up

and start skating. Look, like this."

Ted put his arms above his head and spun round.

Lenny laughed. "That's easy on land," he said, "but it's harder on ice. My feet keep slipping." Slowly, Lenny tried to stand up, but just as he was putting one foot carefully on to the ice, he heard a loud crack!

Chapter 3

The ice was beginning to crack.

"What shall I do?" yelled Lenny.

"Keep still," shouted Ted.

But the ice gave way

and Lenny fell in.

Lenny sank down into darkness. Icy cold water

filled his nose and mouth and he began to choke.

He kicked to push himself back to the top.

He clung to the edge of the ice, gulping in air.

"Don't move," shouted Ted. "I'll go and get help."

"I can't hold on much longer," cried Lenny.

"You've got to help me now!"

Ted looked around for something he could use.

He spotted the branch. Grabbing it, Ted lay down

at the edge of the pond and held it out to Lenny.

"Here," shouted Ted. "Hold on as tight as you can."

Lenny grabbed the branch. Ted pulled and pulled,
but he couldn't pull Lenny out of the water.

Just then the boys heard a voice.

"Come back here!" It was Pete calling his dog.

"Help, Pete, help us!" shouted Ted.

Pete ran over. He grabbed hold of the branch too,
and together they pulled Lenny out
of the water.

"Didn't you read the sign?" said Pete. "The pond might look frozen over but the ice is often thin in the middle."

"Let's get you two home," said Pete. "Come on."

"Mum's going to be so cross," said Lenny, miserably.

"I'll never be allowed out again."

Pete laughed. "Maybe she'll just keep you in until

spring," he said. "At least the ice will have melted

by then!"

Things to think about

1. Why does Lenny's mum tell him to stay away from the pond?
2. Why does Lenny think the ice is safe to walk on?
3. Why do you think Lenny is lucky at the end of the story?
4. What does Pete explain about the ice on the pond?
5. What lesson do you think Lenny might have learned?

Write it yourself

One of the themes in this story is keeping safe. Now try to write your own story about a similar theme.

Plan your story before you begin to write it.
Start off with a story map:
• a beginning to introduce the characters and where your story is set (the setting);
• a problem which the main characters will need to fix in the story;
• an ending where the problems are resolved.

Get writing! Try to use interesting noun phrases such as "icy cold water" to describe your story world and excite your reader.

Notes for parents and carers

Independent reading
This series is designed to provide an opportunity for your child to read independently, for pleasure and enjoyment. These notes are written for you to help your child make the most of this book.

About the book
Lenny and Ted are off to explore the icy woods on their bikes. Lenny's mum has warned him not to go anywhere near the pond, but he is sure the ice is thick enough to walk on. He is lucky to be saved by his neighbour when the ice cracks and he falls in.

Before reading
Ask your child why they have selected this book. Look at the title and blurb together. What do they think it will be about? Do they think they will like it?

During reading
Encourage your child to read independently. If they get stuck on a word, remind them that they can sound it out in syllable chunks. They can also read on in the sentence and think about what would make sense.

After reading
Support comprehension and help your child think about the messages in the book that go beyond the story, using the questions on the page opposite.
Give your child a chance to respond to the story, asking:
Did you enjoy the story and why?
Who was your favourite character?
What was your favourite part?
What did you expect to happen at the end?

Franklin Watts
First published in Great Britain in 2018
by The Watts Publishing Group

Series Editors: Jackie Hamley and Melanie Palmer
Series Advisors: Dr Sue Bodman and Glen Franklin
Series Designer: Peter Scoulding

A CIP catalogue record for this book is
available from the British Library.

ISBN 978 1 4451 6281 2 (hbk)
ISBN 978 1 4451 6283 6 (pbk)
ISBN 978 1 4451 6282 9 (library ebook)

Printed in China

Franklin Watts
An imprint of
Hachette Children's Group
Part of The Watts Publishing Group
Carmelite House
50 Victoria Embankment
London EC4Y 0DZ

An Hachette UK Company
www.hachette.co.uk

www.franklinwatts.co.uk